THE THREE BEARS

Illustrated by

ROBIN SPOWART

ALFRED A. KNOPF 🐎 NEW YORK

This is a Borzoi Book published by Alfred A. Knopf, Inc.

Illustrations copyright © 1987 by Robin Spowart
All rights reserved under International and Pan-American Copyright Conventions.
Published in the United States by Alfred A. Knopf, Inc., New York,
and simultaneously in Canada by Random House of Canada Limited, Toronto.
Distributed by Random House, Inc., New York.
Manufactured in Singapore
2 4 6 8 10 9 7 5 3 1

Library of Congress Cataloging-in-Publication Data
Spowart, Robin. The three bears. Summary: Lost in the woods, a tired and
hungry girl finds the house of the three bears where she helps herself to food and
goes to sleep. [1. Folklore. 1. Bears—Folklore] I. Title.
PZ8.1.S7675Th 1987 [398.2] [E] 86-27322
ISBN 0-394-88862-6 ISBN 0-394-98862-0 (lib. bdg.)

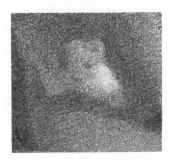

To Alex Spowart

ONCE UPON A TIME there were three bears who lived together in a house of their own in the woods. One of them was a wee little bear, and one was a middle-sized bear, and the other was a great big bear.

They each had a bowl for their porridge—a little bowl for the wee little bear, a middle-sized bowl for the middle-sized bear, and a great big bowl for the great big bear. And they each had a chair to sit in—a little chair for the wee little bear, a middle-sized chair for the middle-sized bear, and a great big chair for the great big bear. And they each had a bed to sleep in—a little bed for the wee little bear, a middle-sized bed for the middle-sized bear, and a great big bed for the great big bear.

One day, after they had made the porridge for their breakfast and had poured it into their bowls, they walked out into the woods while the porridge was cooling. And while they were away a little girl called Goldilocks, who lived on the other side of the woods and who had been sent on an errand by her mother, passed by the house.

First she looked in the window, then she peeped in the keyhole, and
then, seeing nobody inside the house, she lifted the latch on the door.
The door was not locked, because the bears were good bears who never
harmed anyone or suspected that anyone would harm them. So
Goldilocks opened the door and went in.

When she saw the porridge on the table, she was very happy and started to help herself.

First she tasted the porridge of the great big bear, and that was too hot for her. Next she tasted the porridge of the middle-sized bear, but that was too cold for her. And then she tasted the porridge of the wee little bear, and that was neither too hot nor too cold but just right, and she liked it so much that she ate it all up, every bit.

Then Goldilocks, who was tired, sat down in the chair of the great big bear, but that was too hard for her. And then she sat down in the chair of the middle-sized bear, and that was too soft for her. And then she sat down in the chair of the wee little bear, and that was neither too hard nor too soft but just right. So she seated herself in it, and there she sat until the bottom of the chair came out, and down she fell—*plump!*—upon the ground.

Then Goldilocks, who wanted to rest, went upstairs to the bedroom where the three bears slept. And first she lay down upon the bed of the great big bear, but that was too high for her. Next she lay down upon the bed of the middle-sized bear, and that was too low for her. And next she

lay down upon the bed of the wee little bear, and that was neither too high nor too low but just right. So she covered herself up and lay there till she fell fast asleep.

By this time the three bears thought their porridge would be cool enough for them to eat, so they came home to breakfast. Now, Goldilocks had left the spoon of the great big bear in his porridge.

"Somebody has been eating my porridge!" said the great big bear in his great, rough, gruff voice.

Then the middle-sized bear looked at her porridge and saw that her spoon was in it too.

"Somebody has been eating my porridge!" said the middle-sized bear in her middle-sized voice.

Then the wee little bear looked at his porridge, and there was his spoon, but the porridge was all gone.

"Somebody has been eating my porridge and has eaten it all up!" said the wee little bear in his wee little voice.

Upon seeing that someone had entered their house and had eaten up the wee little bear's breakfast, the three bears began to look around them. Now, Goldilocks had not put the hard cushion straight when she rose from the chair of the great big bear.

"Somebody has been sitting in my chair!" said the great big bear in his great, rough, gruff voice.

And Goldilocks had squashed down the soft cushion of the middle-sized chair.

"Somebody has been sitting in my chair!" said the middle-sized bear in her middle-sized voice.

"Somebody has been sitting in my chair and has sat the bottom out of it!" said the wee little bear in his wee little voice.

Then the three bears thought that they had better make a further search, in case it was a burglar, so they went upstairs to their bedroom. Now, Goldilocks had pulled the pillow of the great big bed out of its place.

"Somebody has been lying in my bed!" said the great big bear in his great, rough, gruff voice.

And Goldilocks had pulled the quilt of the middle-sized bed out of its place.

"Somebody has been lying in my bed!" said the middle-sized bear in her middle-sized voice.

But when the wee little bear came to look at his bed, there was the quilt in its place, and the pillow was in its place, and on the pillow was Goldilocks's yellow head—which was not in its place, for she had no business there.

"Somebody has been lying in my bed—and here she is!" said the wee little bear in his wee little voice.

Goldilocks had heard in her sleep the great, rough, gruff voice of the great big bear, but she was so fast asleep that it was no more to her than the roaring of wind or the rumbling of thunder. And she had heard the middle-sized voice of the middle-sized bear, but it was only as if she had heard someone speaking in a dream. But when she heard the wee little voice of the wee little bear, it was so sharp and so shrill that it awakened her at once.

Up she started, and when she saw the three bears on one side of the bed, she tumbled herself out of the other and ran to the window.

Now, the window was open because the bears always opened their bedroom window when they got up in the morning. So Goldilocks jumped. And whether she ran into the woods and was lost there or found her way out and got spanked for being bad, no one can say. But the three bears never saw anything more of her.